For Steven, Susan and Fiona
L.G.

For Tomás
J.S.

EGMONT

We bring stories to life

First published in Great Britain 2018 by Egmont UK Limited,
The Yellow Building, 1 Nicholas Road, London W11 4AN
www.egmont.co.uk

Text copyright © Louise Greig 2018
Illustrations copyright © Júlia Sardà 2018

Louise Greig and Júlia Sardà have asserted their moral rights.

ISBN 978 1 4052 8377 9

A CIP catalogue record for this title is available from the British Library.

Sweep

Louise Greig

Illustrated by Júlia Sardà

EGMONT

Ed in a good mood is a very nice Ed.

Ed in a bad mood is not.

And Ed was in a bad mood.

Not one of those tiny whirlwinds in a teacup
that blow over before they have even begun.

No, this mood swept over him in a raging storm and stuck.

It began as something small . . .

really small, hardly a thing at all.

But before Ed knew it, the something had grown, gathered pace, and swept him off down a path.

Ed's bad mood thought this was a wonderful idea.

But the things that got in Ed's way did not.

Ed knew perfectly well when he had gone far enough,

but he could not bring himself to say, *Okay, that will do.*

So, on he stormed a bit further. And a bit further still.

Until, suddenly the whole thing became **bigger** than him!

Of course, if Ed had looked up he would
have noticed the **beautiful things**,
the things that always made his heart sing.

But he refused to lift his eyes.
The ground was a lot more interesting,
or so his bad mood told him.

Everything seemed against him.

But that just made him even
more determined.

He dug in his heels
and kept going.

Just Ed and his **bad mood**.

Is this **really** *worth it?* he asked himself.

Yes, his bad mood decided, though Ed did wonder a little.

Now his bad mood had swept through the whole town.
The birds had stopped singing.
The flowers had disappeared.

This whole thing was affecting everyone and everything.

Good, thought Ed's bad mood,
but really Ed was beginning to wish it had
all blown over like a whirlwind in a teacup.

Everything grew dark and Ed was getting tired and hungry.
He was finding it harder and harder to keep this up.

Surely he could not give up now?
Not when he had gone to all this trouble.
That would be crazy.

But **something** had to change.

And then something
did change.

A new wind whipped up.

It began as something small,

really small,

that became bigger,

bigger
than Ed.

Suddenly everything looked different.
The world looked **brighter**.

For a moment Ed felt rather silly.
Had he **really** gone to all that effort for nothing?

But at least it had
cleared the air.

It had even blown something his way.

Something that made him look up.

It lifted his mood.
Higher and higher – up to the sky.

And suddenly he noticed beauty all around him.

It swept him away.

As for his bad mood, it vanished into thin air.

Now, when it looks as if Ed might,
just **might**, spiral into a bad mood
and sweep down **that path** again,

he thinks twice.

His first thought is *Will I?*

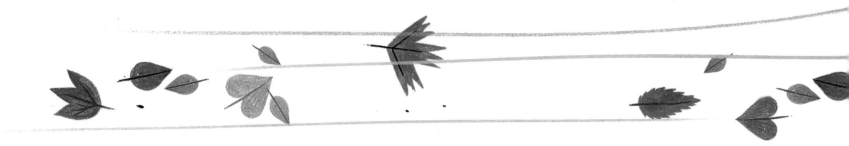

and his second thought is . . .

Or not?